AF584308

For Geoff and Mary – MS

Scholastic Australia
An imprint of Scholastic Australia Pty Limited
PO Box 579 Gosford NSW 2250
ABN 11 000 614 577
www.scholastic.com.au

Part of the Scholastic Group
Sydney · Auckland · New York · Toronto · London · Mexico City
New Delhi · Hong Kong · Buenos Aires · Puerto Rico

Published by Scholastic Australia in 2024.

A catalogue record for this book is available from the National Library of Australia

ISBN: 978-1-76129-455-6

Typeset in Lomba, Suntea, Hank BT, Raski, LunchBox, Pacific Northwest Letters, Mr Happy, Qiber, Candy Randy, PersonalManifesto, Mozzart Sketch, Handserif, Old Claude, YWFT Neighborhood and Mrs Eaves.
Printed in China by Toppan Leefung Printing Ltd.

Scholastic Australia's policy, in association with Toppan Leefung, is to use papers that are renewable and made efficiently with wood from responsibly managed sources, so as to minimise its environmental footprint.

10 9 8 7 6 5 4 3 2 1 24 25 26 27 28 / 2

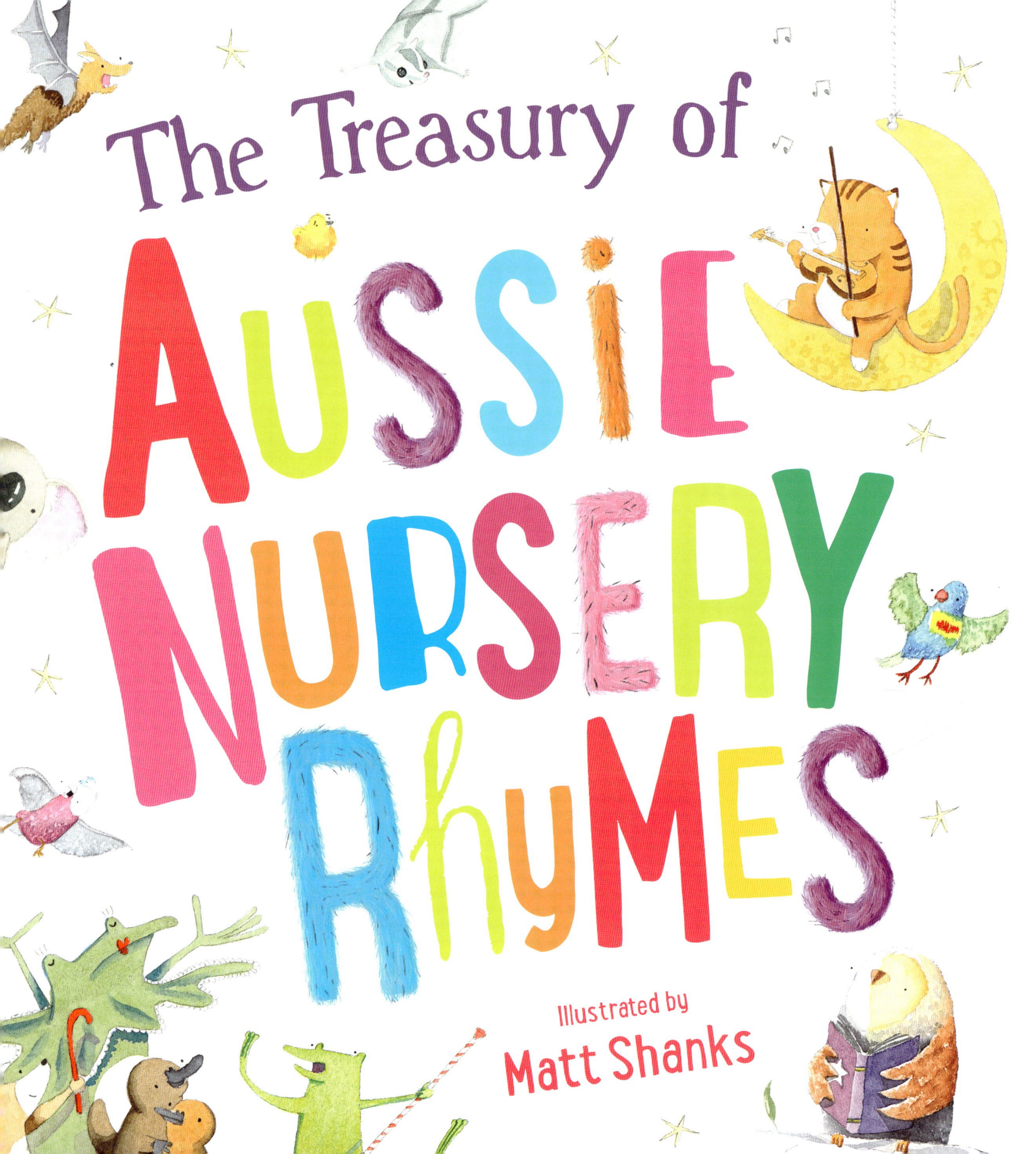
The Treasury of
AUSSIE
NURSERY
RHYMES
Illustrated by
Matt Shanks

CONTENTS

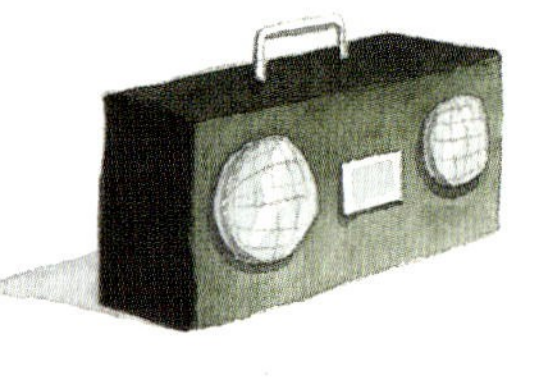

Row, Row, Row Your Boat

Row, row, row your boat,
Swiftly down the creek,
If you see a bandicoot,

Don't forget to **squeak!**

Row, row, row your boat,
High upon the tide,
If you see a platypus,

Don't forget to hide!

Row, row, row your boat,
Slowly by the path,
If you see a kookaburra,

Don’t forget to **laugh!**

Row, row, row your boat,
Further down the stream,
If you see a crocodile,

Don't forget to **scream!**

Row, row, row your boat,
Rocking to and fro,

If your boat rocks too much…

Into the water you go!

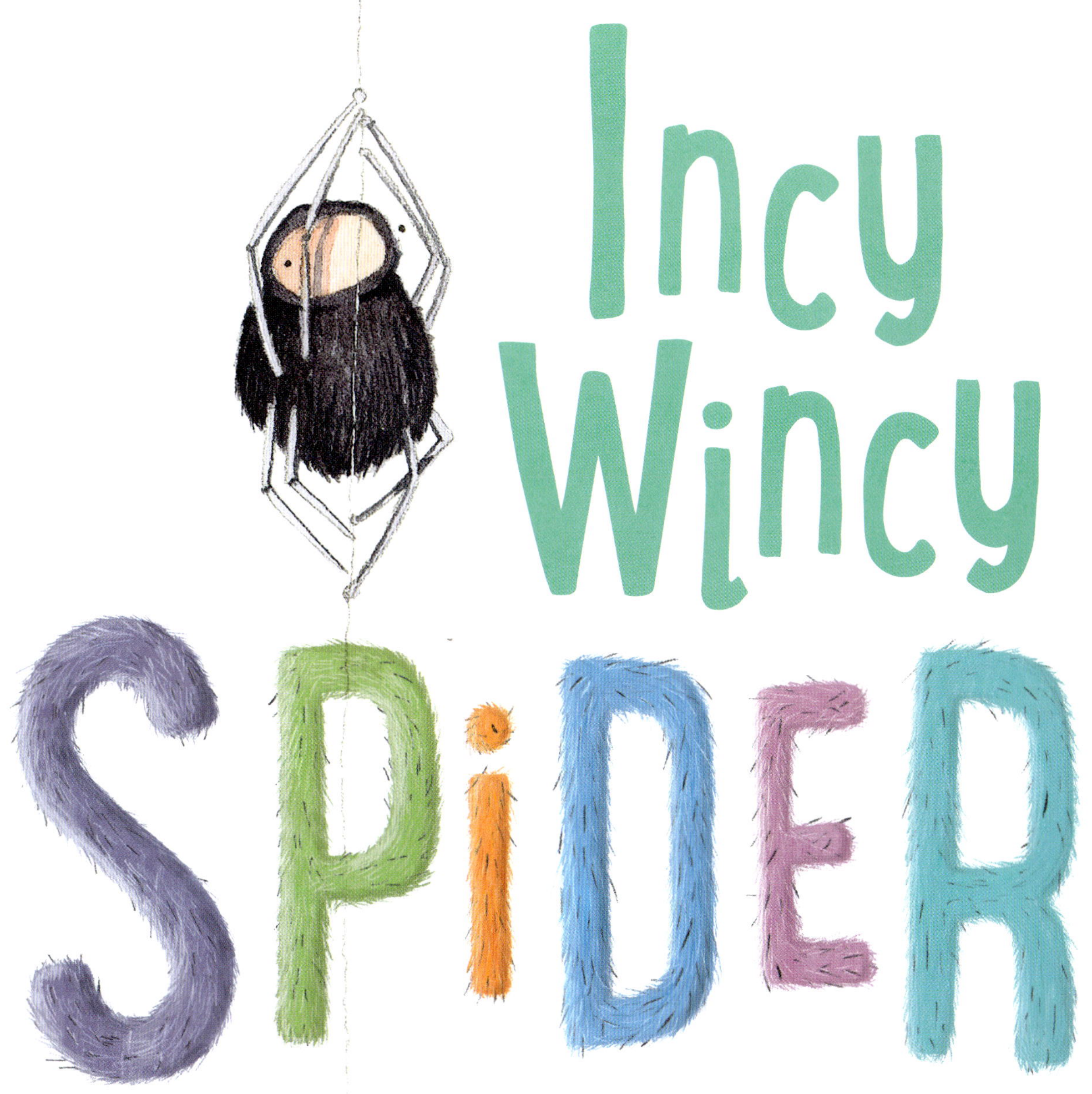
Incy Wincy
SPiDER

Incy Wincy spider climbed up the waterspout.
Down came the rain and
washed the spider out.

Out came the sun and dried up all the rain.
So Incy Wincy spider
climbed up the spout again.

Incy Wincy spider climbed up the bumpy wall.

Swoosh went the wind and made poor Incy fall.

The breeze calmed down until it did not blow,
Then Incy Wincy spider had another go.

Incy Wincy spider climbed up the spiky bale.

Bounce came a roo

and swished her

with his tail!

Down slouched the kangaroo and fell fast asleep.
So Incy Wincy spider back up the bale did creep.

Incy Wincy spider climbed into the bath.
Along came a galah and made the spider laugh.

Then came a **splash** and she went for a ride,
So Incy Wincy spider climbed up the other side.

Incy Wincy spider climbed up onto the chair.

She **tickled** my arm and then she tickled my hair!

Incy wiggled her legs and she wiggled her toes,
Then Incy Wincy spider tickled
my nose!
HA-HA-HA!

Incy Wincy spider climbed up to such a height.

Up **popped** an emu and gave her quite a fright!

Down fell the spider; the emu fled so fast.
So Incy Wincy spider climbed up high at last.

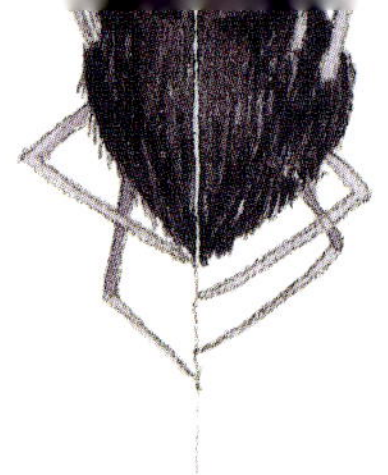

Incy Wincy spider climbed up without a stop.
Then she spun a silky web at the very top.

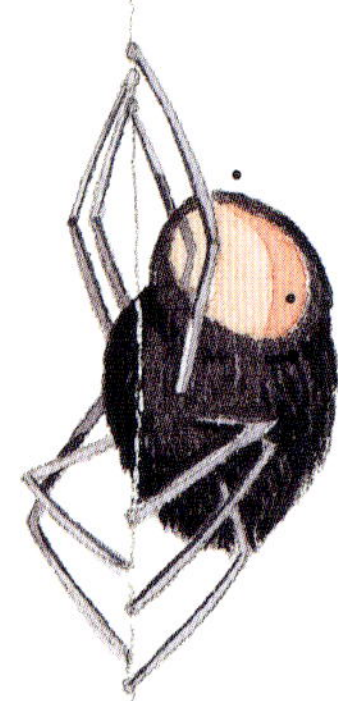

Incy wove and spun and when her web was done . . .

Incy Wincy spider went to sleep
in the sun.

Head, Shoulders, Knees and Toes

Head and shoulders, knees and toes,
Knees and toes, knees and toes,
Head and shoulders, knees and toes,

We all **clap** hands together!

Head and shoulders, knees and . . .
tail!
Knees and tail, knees and tail,
Head and shoulders, knees and tail,

We all **swing** round together!

Eyes and ears and mouth and . . . **scales!**
Mouth and scales, mouth and scales,
Eyes and ears and mouth and scales,

We all go **snap** together!

Head and shoulders, knees and . . . **claws!**
Knees and claws, knees and claws,
Head and shoulders, knees and claws,

We all **stretch** down together!

Eyes and ears and mouth and . . . **paws!**
Mouth and paws, mouth and paws,
Eyes and ears and mouth and paws,

We all **run fast** together!

Head and shoulders, knees and toes,
Knees and toes, knees and toes,

Head and shoulders, knees and toes . . .

We all clap hands **together!**

Der GLUMPH
WENT
THE
LITTLE GREEN FROG

Der glumph went the little green frog one day.

Der glumph went the little green frog.

Der glumph went the little green frog one day.

And they all went

der glumph,

der glumph,

der glumph!

BUT . . .

We all know frogs go la-di-da-di-da!

La-di-da-di-da! La-di-da-di-da!

We all know frogs go la-di-da-di-da!

They don't go

der glumph, der glumph, der glumph!

Scritch, scratch went the spiky echidna one day.

Scritch, scratch went the spiky echidna.

Scritch, scratch went the spiky echidna one day.

And they all went

scritchy,

scratch,

scratch!

BUT . . .

We all know echidnas go roly-poly-roll!

Roly-poly-roll! Roly-poly-roll!

We all know echidnas go roly-poly-roll!

They don't go

scritchy, scratch, scratch!

Snug-hug went the fluffy penguin one day.

Snug-hug went the fluffy penguin.

Snug-hug went the fluffy penguin one day.

And they all went

snuggy-hug-hug!

We all know penguins go flippy-flappy-flap!

Flippy-flappy-flap!
Flippy-flappy-flap!

We all know penguins go flippy-flappy-flap!

They don't go

snuggy-hug-hug!

Hop, hop went the little red roo one day.

Hop, hop went the little red roo.

Hop, hop went the little red roo one day.

And they all went

hop, hop, hop!

We all know roos go boingy-boingy-boing!

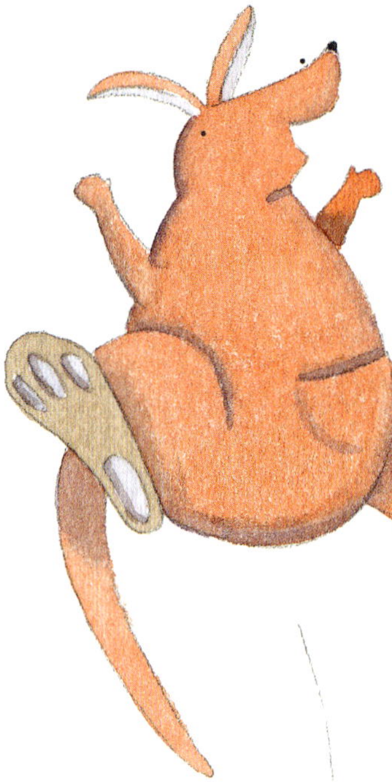

Boingy-boingy-boing! Boingy-boingy-boing!

We all know roos go boingy-boingy-boing!

They don't go **hop, hop, hop!**

Chomp, chomp went the spotty brown turtle one day.

Chomp, chomp went the spotty brown turtle.

Chomp, chomp went the spotty brown turtle one day.

And they all went

chomp,

chomp,

chomp!

We all know turtles go slippy-slippy-slide!

Slippy-slippy-slide!
Slippy-slippy-slide!

We all know turtles go slippy-slippy-slide!

They don't go

chomp, chomp, chomp!

Squawky-squawk went the little pink bird one day.

Squawky-squawk went the little pink bird.

Squawky-squawk went the little pink bird one day.

And they all went

squawky-squawk-squawk!

We all know birds go la-di-da-di-da!

La-di-da-di-da! La-di-da-di-da!

We all know birds go la-di-da-di-da . . .

They don't go

squawky-squawk-squawk!

Old
MacDonald
had a
FARM

Old MacDonald had a farm,

e-i-e-i-o.

And on that farm he had a 'roo,

e-i-e-i-o.

With a **boing-boing** here

and a **boing-boing** there.

Here a **boing**,

there a **boing**,

everywhere a **boing-boing**!

Old MacDonald had a farm,

e-i-e-i-o.

Old MacDonald had a farm,

e-i-e-i-o.

And on that farm he had a koala,

e-i-e-i-o.

With a **munch-munch** here
and a **munch-munch** there.
Here a **munch**,
there a **munch**,
everywhere a **munch-munch**!

Old MacDonald had a farm,
e-i-e-i-o.

Old MacDonald had a farm,

e-i-e-i-o.

And on that farm he had a wombat,

e-i-e-i-o.

With a **dig-dig** here

and a **dig-dig** there.

Here a **dig**,

there a **dig**,

everywhere a **dig-dig**!

Old MacDonald had a farm,

e-i-e-i-o.

Old MacDonald had a farm,

e-i-e-i-o.

And on that farm he had a cockatoo,

e-i-e-i-o.

With a **screech-screech** here

and a **screech-screech** there.

Here a **screech**,

there a **screech**,

everywhere a **screech-screech**!

Old MacDonald had a farm,

e-i-e-i-o.

Old MacDonald had a farm,

e-i-e-i-o.

And on that farm he had a platypus,

e-i-e-i-o.

With a **dive-dive** here

and a **dive-dive** there.

Here a **dive**,

there a **dive**,

everywhere a **dive-dive**!

Old MacDonald had a farm,

e-i-e-i-o.

Old MacDonald had a farm,

e-i-e-i-o.

And on that farm he had an emu,

e-i-e-i-o.

With a **peck-peck** here

and a **peck-peck** there.

Here a **peck**,

there a **peck**,

everywhere a

peck-
peck!

Old MacDonald had a farm,

e-i-e-i-o.

Twinkle, Twinkle, Little Star

Twinkle, twinkle, little star,
How I wonder what you are!

Up above the world so high,
Like a diamond in the sky.
Twinkle, twinkle, little star,
How I wonder what you are!

When the blazing sun is gone,
When he nothing shines upon,

Then you show your little light,
Twinkle, twinkle, all the night.

Then the traveller in the dark,
Thanks you for your tiny spark,

He could not see which way to go,
If you did not twinkle so.

In the dark blue sky you keep,
And often through my curtains peep,
For you never shut your eye,
Till the sun is in the sky.

As your bright and tiny spark,
Lights the traveller in the dark,
Though I know not what you are,
Twinkle, twinkle, little star.

Twinkle, twinkle, little star,
How I wonder what you are!

ROUND and
ROUND
the GARDEN

Round and round the **garden,**

like a teddy bear.

One step.

Two steps.

Tickle you under there!

Round and round the **wattle tree,**

like a lorikeet.

One flap.

Two flaps.

Dance to the beat!

Round and round the **river**,

like a crocodile.

One snap.

Two snaps.

Give a great big smile!

Round and round the **bottlebrush**,

like a sugar glider.

One leap.

Two leaps.

Stretch your arms out wider!

Round and round the **mountains,**

like a wild brumby.

One jump.

Two jumps.

Rub your little tummy!

Round and round the **campfire,**

like a big wombat.

One dig.

Two digs.

Give your head a pat!

Round and round the **gum tree,**

like a koala off to sleep.

One blink.

Two blinks.

Now do not make a peep!

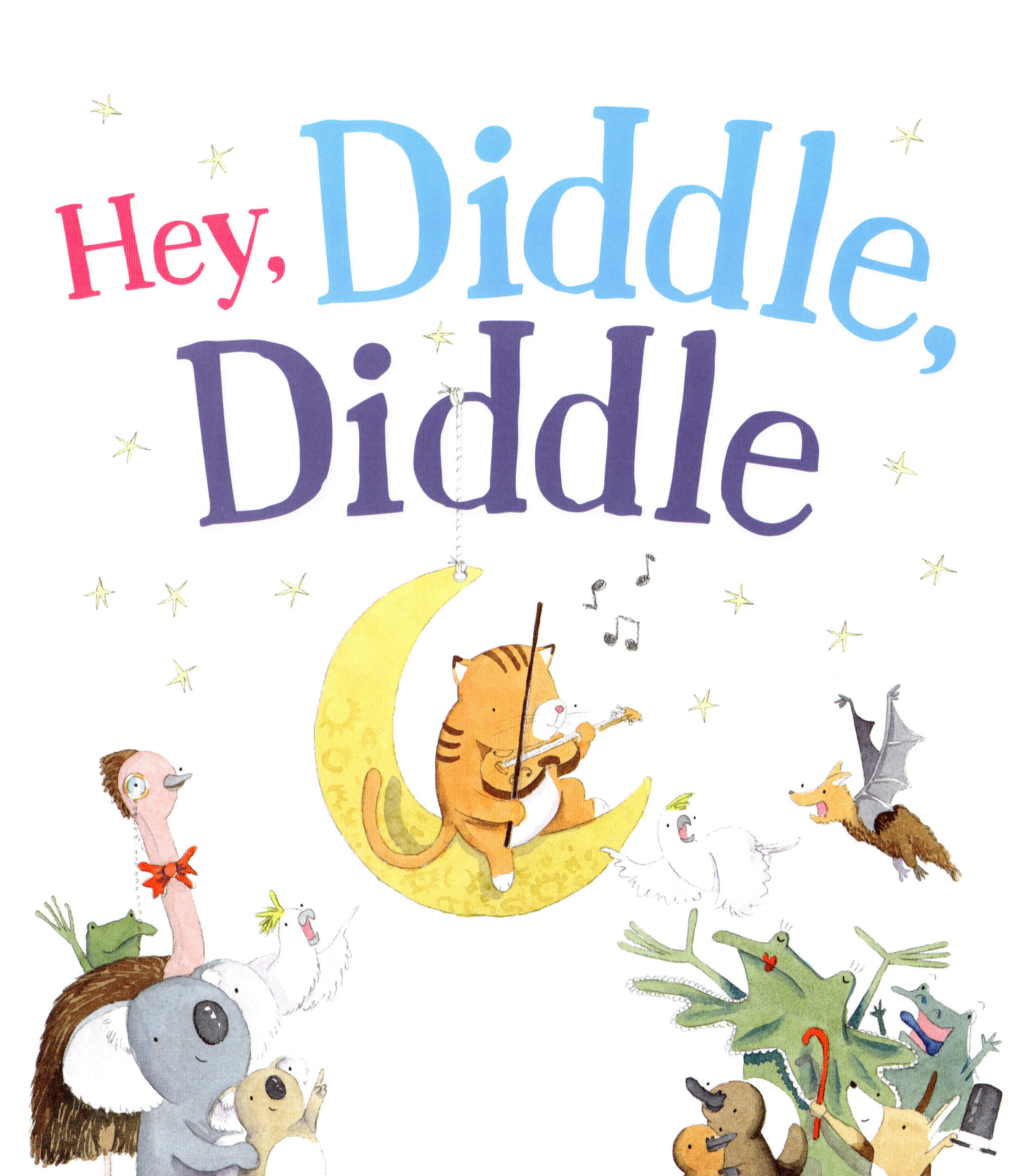
Hey, Diddle, Diddle

Hey, diddle, doddle,
the goannas waddle,
the frog sprang onto the box;

the wallabies clap
their paws in glee,
as the croc flips round the flying fox.

Hey, diddle, duddle,
the koalas cuddle,
the dingo howls loud and slow;
the echidna twirls
all by himself,
and the glow worms put on quite a show.

Hey, diddle, dwiddle,
frill-neck's in the middle
as she takes up the spotlight;

the animals dance
across the grass,
and agree it's a fabulous night.

1
2
3

Hey, diddle, deddle,
the snake wins a medal,
the blue-tongue gets second place;

the pussy cat sings
to end the show,
and all leave with a smile on their face.

GLOSSARY OF AUSSIE ANIMALS

Galah
Owl
Glow-worm
Possum
Kookaburra
Emu
Platypus
Sugar Glider
Wombat
Goanna
Crocodile
Penguin

ABOUT THE ILLUSTRATOR

Matt Shanks

Matt Shanks is a critically acclaimed author/illustrator. He was born in Australia, but his father comes from the land of badgers and foxes (England), and his mother, the land of witches and bears (Croatia). Now that he's all grown up in a land of echidnas and koalas, kangaroos and crocodiles, it seems only fitting that he combine his love for these unique Australian animals with the rhymes of his childhood that were born overseas. He believes deeply in the power of books, stories and songs to help bring people together, and he hopes this book will do just that. Matt works primarily in watercolour but often mixes it with a dash of humour and plenty of fun.

Matt acknowledges the traditional custodians of the land on which he does his work—the Bunurong people of the South-Eastern Kulin Nation—and pays his respects to elders past and present.

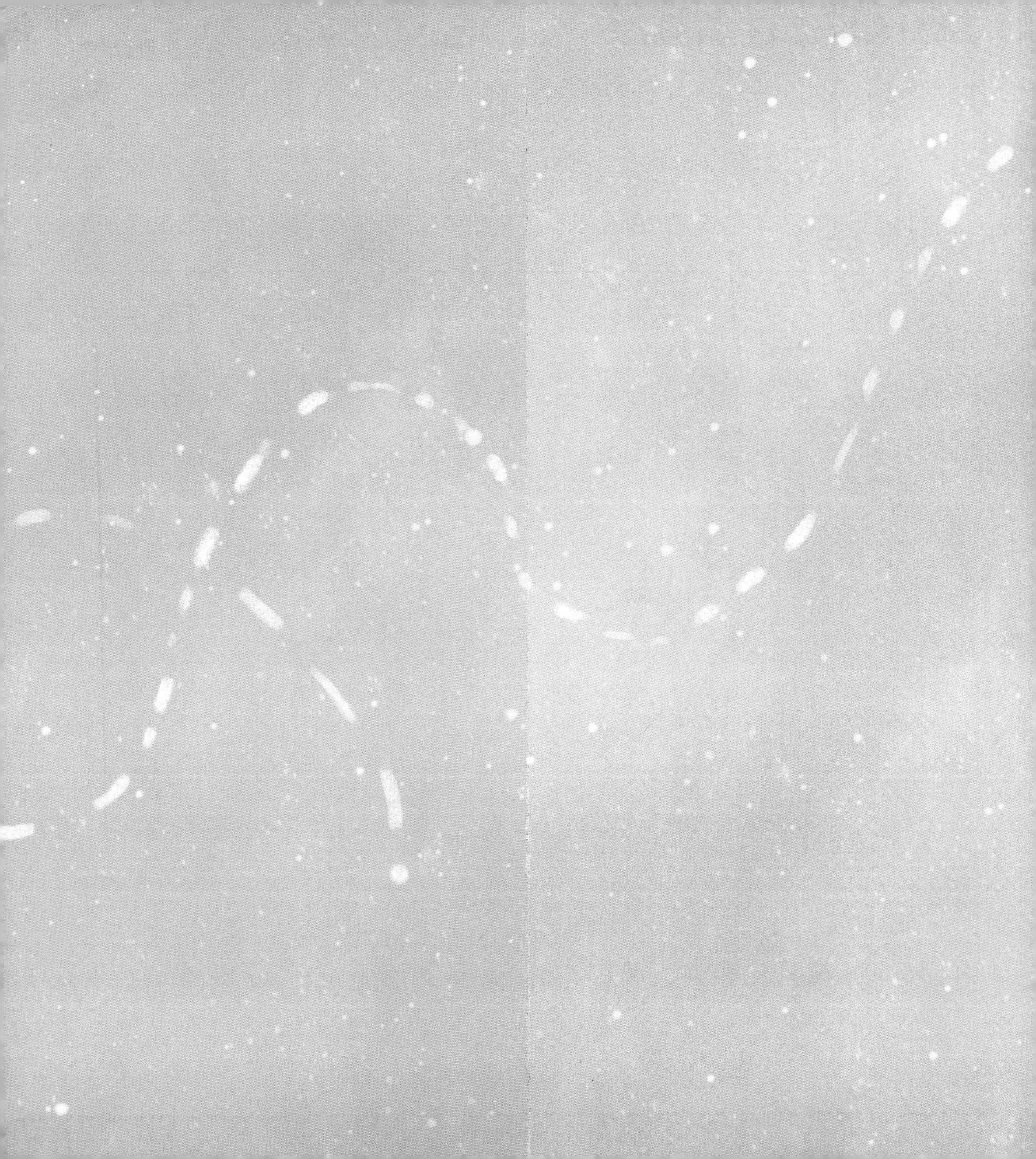